THE MOST MAGNiFICENT MAKER'S

A to Z

Some words to remember
for little makers everywhere.

Published in Canada and the U.S. by Kids Can Press Ltd.
25 Dockside Drive, Toronto, ON M5A 0B5

Kids Can Press is a Corus Entertainment Inc. company
www.kidscanpress.com

D is for digitally. Which is how the artwork in this book was rendered. The text is set in Bookeyed Nelson.

Edited by Yasemin Uçar
Designed by Karen Powers

Printed and bound in
Malaysia in 6/2023
CM 23 0 9 8 7 6 5 4 3 2

LIBRARY AND ARCHIVES CANADA CATALOGUING IN PUBLICATION

Title: The most magnificent maker's A to Z / written and illustrated by Ashley Spires.

Names: Spires, Ashley, 1978- author, illustrator.

Identifiers: Canadiana (print) 20220468559 | Canadiana (ebook) 20220469172 | ISBN 9781525306297 (hardcover) | ISBN 9781525308871 (EPUB)

Subjects: LCSH: Makerspaces—Juvenile literature. | LCSH: Handicraft—Juvenile literature. | LCSH: Science projects—Juvenile literature. | LCSH: Alphabet books. | LCGFT: Picture books. | LCGFT: Alphabet books.

Classification: LCC TS171.57 .S65 2023 | DDC j600—dc23

Kids Can Press gratefully acknowledges that the land on which our office is located is the traditional territory of many nations, including the Mississaugas of the Credit, the Anishnabeg, the Chippewa, the Haudenosaunee and the Wendat peoples, and is now home to many diverse First Nations, Inuit and Métis peoples.

We thank the Government of Ontario, through Ontario Creates, the Ontario Arts Council; the Canada Council for the Arts; and the Government of Canada for supporting our publishing activity.

THE MOST MAGNIFiCENT MAKER'S A to Z

Written and illustrated by
Ashley Spires

KIDS CAN PRESS

 is for A GIRL and her ASSISTANT,
who love to make magnificent things together.

B is for BRAINSTORM.
When ideas of all shapes
and sizes rain onto the page.

is for DESK.
A special, out-of-the-way place
where you can get to work.

 is for EXPERIMENT.

Test it out.

Try it different ways.

Maybe there is a best way that you haven't discovered yet.

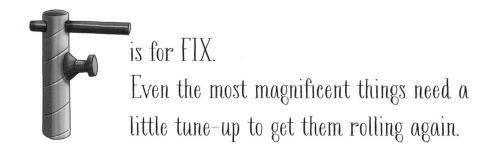

is for FIX.
Even the most magnificent things need a
little tune-up to get them rolling again.

 is for GATHERING SUPPLIES.
Don't forget your scrap paper, ruler, glue,
pencil, paint, googly eyes, screwdriver,
egg cartons, 3D printer, vacuum cleaner...

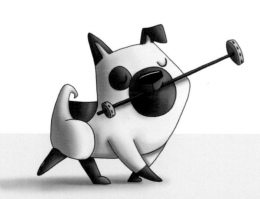

maybe just bring everything!

is for HELP.
Sometimes we all need an
extra set of hands. Or paws.

 is for IDEA.
A gift from the imagination
that wants to be made.

is for JUST ABOUT.
It's a bit crooked, sort of wobbly
and could use another coat of
paint, but you've almost got it.

 is for KEEP GOING.

Making things is an adventure full of ups and downs.

Don't give up!

 is for LEARN.

Do some research.

New information will feed your brain and fuel your creativity.

 is for MISTAKES.
They happen ... A LOT.
And they help us get even better.

N is for NOTEBOOK.
A home for ideas that you can bring anywhere.

 is for OLD OBJECTS.
With a little imagination and some tinkering,
discarded items can have a whole new purpose.

is for PATIENCE.

Most things don't work
the first time ...

or the third time ...

or even the twelfth time.

 is for QUESTIONS.
Why isn't it working? What would
make it better? Do you need a snack?

is for RETHINK.

You can't force an idea to work. If it's not clicking, let go of what you've done and try looking at it from a different angle.

 is for STUCK.
Sometimes your idea machine is jammed
and your hands don't know what to do next.

Don't worry, ideas have a way of sneaking
up on you when you aren't looking for them.

T is for TRY, TRY, TRY ...

and TRY AGAIN.

(And after that, TRY some more.)

 is for UNMAKE.
Take it apart. Start over.
Sometimes going backward is
the best way to move forward.

 is for VARIETY.
There are so many ways to make stuff!

Dabble in collage.

Fiddle with clay.

Play with paper cups.

Try them all! Find out how YOU like to make.

 is for WALK AWAY.

If nothing is working, and you're so frustrated that you want to sit down and cry, take a break.

 is for X MARKS THE SPOT.
Straighten, measure, adjust and ... there!
Exactly where it needs to go.

is for YET.
Creating is a journey. You may not have figured it out YET,
but you can try again tomorrow.

Z is for ZILLIONS
of possibilities.

What magnificent thing will
YOU make next?

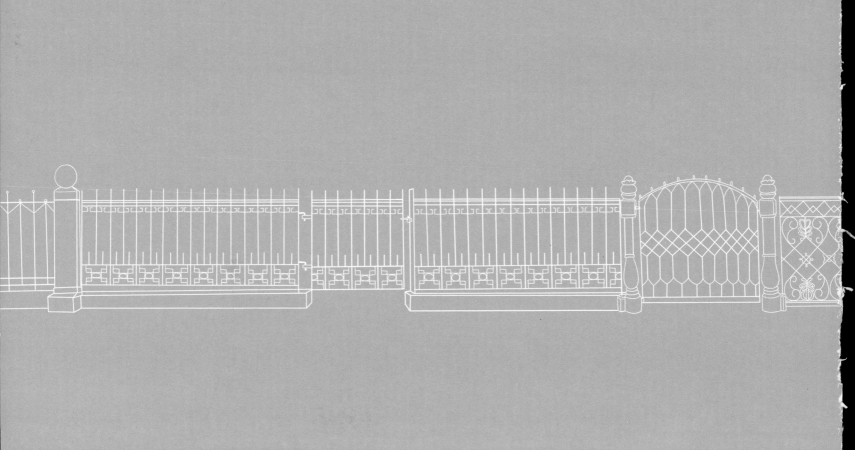